Buses came and went. Yet the two men in the dark suits remained waiting by the railing.

Encyclopedia lost sight of them when passengers, streaming from the two o'clock bus from Glenn City, blocked his view. Suddenly, a woman screamed.

The detectives rushed over. A black-haired man lay on the floor, unconscious. No one seemed to know what had happened to him.

Officer Carlson came hurrying up. "It's Blue-Point Blackie," he said in surprise. "What is a Chicago crook doing in Idaville?"

## ENCYCLOPEDIA BROWN
### and The Case of
### the Midnight Visitor

## HEY, KIDS!

Do you have a wacky story to tell about an animal, a fact, a crime, a sport? The funnier and wackier the better! But it must be *true*.

You can write about it, or enclose a clipping from your local newspaper, or send a note from your parents or teacher verifying the story. If it is included in an Encyclopedia Brown book, your name will appear in the book.

Send your wacky true story (along with your name and address) to: Encyclopedia Brown, c/o Bantam Books, 666 Fifth Avenue, New York 10103.

AMERICA'S SHERLOCK HOLMES IN SNEAKERS · No. 13

# ENCYCLOPEDIA BROWN
## and The Case of
## the Midnight Visitor

## By DONALD J. SOBOL

## Illustrated by Lillian Brandi

BANTAM BOOKS · TORONTO · NEW YORK · LONDON

## A BANTAM SKYLARK BOOK

ENCYCLOPEDIA BROWN AND
THE CASE OF THE MIDNIGHT VISITOR
A Bantam Skylark Book/published by arrangement with
Elsevier/Nelson Books

PRINTING HISTORY

Elsevier/Nelson edition published December 1977
A selection of the Weekly Reader Book Club
Bantam Skylark edition/September 1980

Bantam Books are published by Bantam Books, Inc. Its trademark,
consisting of the words "Bantam Books" and the portrayal of a bantam, is Registered in U.S. Patent and Trademark Office and in other
countries. Marca Registrada. Bantam Books, Inc., 666 Fifth Avenue,
New York, New York 10103.

PRINTED IN THE UNITED STATES OF AMERICA

12  11  10  9  8  7  6  5  4  3

For
Lenore and Jerry Gundersheimer

# Contents

1.  *The Case of the Midnight Visitor*          1

2.  *The Case of the Hidden Penny*          13

3.  *The Case of the Red Sweater*          23

4.  *The Case of the Painting Gerbils*          33

5.  *The Case of the Time Capsule*          43

6.  *The Case of Freddy the Great*          53

7.  *The Case of the Tennis Racket*          63

8.  *The Case of the Fifty Mosquitoes*          73

9.  *The Case of Blue-Point Blackie*          83

10.  *The Case of the Hit-Run Car*          93

# ENCYCLOPEDIA BROWN
## and The Case of
## the Midnight Visitor

# The Case of
# the Midnight Visitor

Now there are some people in the United States who had never heard of Idaville. But they were not policemen.

Every policeman from Maine to California knew about Idaville. Anyone who broke the law there was caught. Not a crook escaped.

How could that be? What was the secret?

No one ever guessed.

Idaville looked like many other seaside towns its size. It had lovely beaches, three movie theaters, and four banks. It had churches, a synagogue, and two delicatessens.

And on Rover Avenue it had a certain red brick house.

In the house lived Idaville's secret weapon against crime—ten-year-old Encyclopedia Brown.

Encyclopedia's father was chief of police. Because no one got away with breaking the law, the people of Idaville thought he was the bravest and smartest police chief in the world.

True, Chief Brown was brave. And he was smart enough to know what to do with a case he could not solve.

He took it home to dinner.

Over soup, he told his son the facts. Encyclopedia usually figured out the answer before dessert.

Chief Brown hated keeping the help he got from his only child a secret. He wanted Encyclopedia's sneakers hung in the Crime Fighters' Hall of Fame.

But what good would it do to suggest it?

Who would take him seriously? Who would believe that the mastermind behind Idaville's spotless police record was a fifth grader?

So Chief Brown said nothing.

Encyclopedia never mentioned the help he gave his father. He didn't want to seem different from other boys.

There was nothing he could do about his nickname, however.

Only his parents and teachers called him by his real name, Leroy. Everyone else called him Encyclopedia.

An encyclopedia is a book or set of books filled with facts from A to Z. So was Encyclopedia's head. He had read so many books his pals swore his ears were turning into bookends.

Monday evening Chief Brown sipped his soup slowly. Encyclopedia and his mother knew what that meant. He had his mind on a case.

Finally, Mrs. Brown said, "Why don't you tell Leroy about it, dear?"

Chief Brown sighed. "I don't know . . . this is an awfully tough case," he said. "It has me beaten."

"Leroy has never failed you. Tell him," urged Mrs. Brown.

"Very well," said Chief Brown. "C. T. Butler was kidnapped from his home last night."

Mrs. Brown gasped. Encyclopedia let out a low whistle.

C. T. Butler was a millionaire. He owned a string of pizza parlors in three states and a big house by the ocean.

"Today at noon, Mrs. Butler received a phone call," said Chief Brown. "A man's voice said that her husband was un-harmed, but he was being held for half a million dollars' ransom. The caller told Mrs. Butler to remain home tomorrow, at which time she would be told by phone where to leave the money."

"You hope to capture the kidnappers before they are paid the ransom, Dad?" said Encyclopedia.

"We must," replied Chief Brown grimly. "Kidnappers want money. Once they get it, there is no telling what they might do to their victim."

"Poor Mr. Butler!" exclaimed Mrs. Brown. "Well, at least you have until to-morrow to find him."

"That's too little time," said Chief Brown.

"Somebody must have heard or seen *something*," said Encyclopedia.

"Mrs. Butler was of some help," said Chief Brown. "From what she told me, it's possible to fit together a few pieces."

He took a spoonful of soup. Then he related all that the police had been able to learn about the kidnapping.

"Last night, Mr. and Mrs. Butler were in bed watching a late movie on television. A little after midnight, the front doorbell rang.

"Mr. Butler went downstairs to see who it was. Mrs. Butler turned off the television and listened. She heard him talking to someone—she thinks a man. She couldn't make out the words, but the tone was friendly.

"Then she heard the sounds of the door closing and footsteps going into the den. Mr. Butler and his visitor lowered their voices. She could scarcely hear them at all.

"She went to sleep. She was awakened by the closing of the front door and then went back to sleep.

"When she awoke this morning, Mr. Butler wasn't in the house. The front door was closed but unlocked."

"Wasn't Mrs. Butler worried?" asked Mrs. Brown.

"No," answered Chief Brown. "She thought her husband had dressed quietly so he wouldn't wake her and had gone to the office. He sometimes forgets to lock the front door behind him. She didn't report him missing until she got the phone call from the kidnapper."

"Wasn't she worried when he didn't return to bed after the visitor left?" said Mrs. Brown.

Chief Brown shook his head. "Mr. Butler often gets up at night to work in his den. She thought he had simply remained downstairs to go over some business."

"You don't have much to work with, dear," said Mrs. Brown.

"We know that whoever came to the door wasn't a stranger," said Chief Brown. "Mr. Butler never would have let a stranger into his house late at night. I think this is what happened.

"The visitor spoke with Mr. Butler in the den. Then he opened the window and made Mr. Butler climb into the back yard, where other men were waiting. They forced Mr. Butler into a car on the dark street and drove away. The visitor left by the front door."

"Wasn't that dangerous?" said Mrs. Brown. "Someone might have seen him under the night light."

"He was probably afraid that he'd been seen entering the house. So he had to be seen leaving. He was prepared to say that Mr. Butler was still in the house when he left. But no one saw him enter or leave."

"Then you really have no clues," said Mrs. Brown glumly.

"Only a calendar," replied Chief Brown.

He got up from the table and returned with his briefcase. He took out a calendar. On it was handwritten in pencil, "7891011."

"Mrs. Butler had been in the den last night with her husband just before they went upstairs to the bedroom," said Chief Brown. "She said nothing was different on his desk this morning but the writing on the calendar. That is, this number."

Chief Brown passed the calendar to Encyclopedia. "Make anything out of it, son?" he inquired.

"My only clue is a calendar," said Chief Brown.

Encyclopedia studied the number and the calendar. He closed his eyes. He always closed his eyes when he did his hardest thinking.

... *7891011* ...

"Does Mr. Butler have any enemies?" asked Mrs. Brown.

"Every wealthy man has enemies," said Chief Brown. "He is known to have argued with Arthur Jason, John McNear, and Matt Short. There are probably a dozen others."

"I argue with my closest friends," objected Mrs. Brown, "and I haven't been kidnapped."

Encyclopedia opened his eyes. He asked his one question. He seldom needed more than one question to break a case that his father brought home to dinner.

"Was there any paper on Mr. Butler's desk?"

"Just a small pad by the telephone," said Chief Brown. "But it was blank."

"Is that a clue, Leroy?" said Mrs. Brown anxiously.

"Yes," said Encyclopedia. "When the visitor went to open the window, Mr. Butler seized the moment to write this number on the calendar."

"What does it mean?" asked Mrs. Brown.

"It tells us the visitor's name," said Encyclopedia. "The rest should be easy, right, Dad?"

## WHAT WAS THE VISITOR'S NAME?

*(Turn to page 103 for the solution to The Case of the Midnight Visitor.)*

# The Case of
# the Hidden Penny

Encyclopedia wanted to help the children of the neighborhood. So when school let out for the summer, he opened his own detective agency in the garage.

Every morning he hung out his sign:

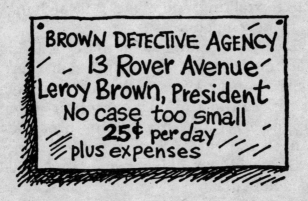

BROWN DETECTIVE AGENCY
13 Rover Avenue
Leroy Brown, President
No case too small
25¢ per day
plus expenses

On Tuesday, business was slow all morning till Elmo Thomas came in. Elmo was Idaville's junior yo-yo champion.

"Mothers," he grumbled. "They don't understand kids."

"That's no way to talk," protested Encyclopedia.

"If my mother understood me, I wouldn't have got kicked in the rear and had my best yo-yo stolen. I'd be worth a lot of money, besides."

"All that is your mother's fault?"

"Well, not really," admitted Elmo. "She just doesn't understand what it takes to be a yo-yo champ. You can't sit back. You have to keep your hand and eye sharp to stay in the big time. You follow me?"

"Keep talking, and maybe I'll catch up," said Encyclopedia.

"Last week I broke a lamp in the living room doing a loop-the-loop," said Elmo. "This morning I was in the kitchen practicing round-the-corner when Mom tripped over the string. Her breakfast went flying."

"She said something to you," guessed Encyclopedia.

"And how. She told me I'd have to practice outdoors. That was mean. It's daylight outdoors."

"You noticed?" said Encyclopedia, blinking.

"I'd planned to work today in the basement with my number-one yo-yo. It glows in the dark," said Elmo. "But I made the best of things. I went outside and put a blanket over my head."

Encyclopedia could scarcely wait to hear what was coming next.

"I was getting pretty good under the blanket," said Elmo. "No fancy stuff like three-leaf-clover or man-on-the-flying-trapeze. Just lots of fast *zzizz thwop!*—till Bugs Meany kicked my backside."

"Oh, boy," said Encyclopedia. "Bugs shows up wherever there is trouble."

Bugs Meany was the leader of a gang of tough older boys. They called themselves the Tigers. They should have called themselves the Taffee Twisters. They were always pulling something crooked.

"After Bugs kicked me, he yanked off the blanket and begged my pardon," recalled Elmo. "He said he thought I was an

"*Bugs Meany kicked my backside while I was practicing my glow-in-the-dark yo-yo,*" *said Elmo.*

Arab. He took my yo-yo and put it in his pocket and asked me my name.

" 'Elmo Thomas,' I said.

"Bugs laughed. 'Go buy yourself a last name,' he said, and flipped me a penny."

"He bought your best yo-yo for one cent?" exclaimed Encyclopedia. "No wonder you're sore."

"Forget the yo-yo," said Elmo. "The penny was dated 1901 and had an *S* mark under the date. It's worth twenty-five dollars or more. Bugs must have seen the look on my face right away. He took back the penny and kept the yo-yo."

Elmo put a quarter on the gas can beside Encyclopedia.

"I want to hire you," he said. "Get back the penny. I figure it belongs to me."

"So do I," said Encyclopedia. "If I know Bugs, he'll have hidden the yo-yo, but he won't let the penny out of his sight. C'mon."

The two boys hurried to the Tigers' clubhouse, an unused tool shed behind Mr. Sweeny's Auto Body shop. The clubhouse was empty.

"When Bugs celebrates a crooked deal,

he usually goes to Friedman's Deli-
catessen for a hot dog and root beer," Encyclopedia said. "The sauerkraut is free.
He's probably there now."

Encyclopedia was correct. Bugs stood
at the relish counter. He had piled sauerkraut two inches high on his hot dog and
roll and was smearing mustard on top
with a wooden spoon.

"Make like a rattlesnake and bite yourself to death," he growled as the boy detective came up.

Encyclopedia was used to Bugs's warm
greeting. "You stole the penny you paid
Elmo for his yo-yo this morning. Give it
back."

"Elmo? Who's Elmo?" gasped Bugs,
looking around.

"Me, you big bully!" said Elmo.

"Man, oh, man!" cried Bugs. "I never
saw this child in my life. I was out in the
woods all morning studying woodpeckers
to find out why they don't get headaches."

He walked toward a table and sat down.
Encyclopedia and Elmo followed.

Bugs leaned over and tightened the lace
on his right shoe. He bit into his hot dog

and chewed, his mouth barely able to close. Then he took a drink of root beer.

"Go on, scram," he said. "I'm eating." He shifted under Encyclopedia's stare and tapped his right foot nervously. "Say, maybe you'd like to search me?"

"Nope," said Encyclopedia.

Bugs shrugged and finished his drink. He tossed the paper cup into a trash can ten feet away.

"I'm going for another soda," he announced. "Be useful and watch my hot dog while I'm gone."

He walked toward the soda counter grinning.

"Why didn't you *search* him?" demanded Elmo.

"Because I know where he's hidden the penny," replied Encyclopedia.

## WHERE?

*(Turn to page 104 for the solution to The Case of the Hidden Penny.)*

# The Case of
# the Red Sweater

Bugs Meany lived for the day when he could get even with Encyclopedia.

Bugs hated being outsmarted all the time. He longed to smack Encyclopedia so hard the boy detective would have to stand on his head to turn things over in his mind.

But Bugs never dared throw a punch.

Whenever he felt like it, he thought of Sally Kimball. Sally was Encyclopedia's partner and the prettiest girl in the fifth grade.

More to the point, she had done what no boy under twelve had believed possible. She had punched out Bugs Meany!

*The skull had two holes in the top. "Bullet holes,"*
*said the girl. "I just know it."*

Whenever they fought, Bugs ended on the ground mumbling about a low bridge.

Because of Sally, Bugs never tried to bully Encyclopedia. But he never stopped planning his day of revenge.

"Bugs hates you as much as me," Encyclopedia said to Sally. "He'll never live down the lickings you gave him."

The two detectives were sitting in the Brown Detective Agency playing checkers. It was a chilly morning. Sally wore a gray sweat shirt and Encyclopedia his red sweater.

Suddenly a girl in a black leather jacket appeared at the door. She was holding a human skull.

The skull had two holes in the top.

"Bullet holes," said the girl. "I just know it."

Encyclopedia studied the holes and shook his head.

"The science department at the high school got a new skeleton last year and threw away the old one," he said. "The skull had two holes in the top where it was hung by wire."

"Where did you find it?" asked Sally.

"In the junkyard an hour ago," answered the girl. "The rest of the skeleton is there."

Encyclopedia had been eager to own a skeleton for some time. He asked the girl to take them to the spot.

During the bike ride, he learned that her name was Carmine Oldfield and that she was new in the neighborhood.

"I heard you were detectives," she said. "I thought I'd better bring the skull straight to you."

When they arrived at the junkyard, Carmine went to the back gate. The lock was broken.

"See that oil drum by the yellow truck?" she asked. "The rest of the skeleton is in there."

The detectives hurried to the oil drum. Inside was a thick sack. Encyclopedia reached down and pulled it out.

"Caught in the act!"

Bugs Meany leaped from behind a pile of wrecked cars. Officer Murphy was at his heels.

"Let me have the sack," said Officer Murphy sharply.

Encyclopedia handed it to the policeman, who opened it upon the ground.

Instead of bones, the sack held pens,
wallets, toy cars, and other small articles.

"Man, oh, man!" sang Bugs. "I broke
Idaville's biggest shoplifting ring!"

"Bugs claims you've been shoplifting at
the Five-and-Dime for months," explained Officer Murphy. "On the way
back from town, you hide your loot here.
He's been tailing you."

"*When* did we shoplift?" demanded
Sally. "Tell me!"

Bugs named days. They were the days
the detectives had biked into town during
the past month.

"Nice try, Bugs," said Encyclopedia.
"But we have a witness, Carmine Oldfield.
Carmine . . . ?"

Carmine was nowhere in sight.

"You put her up to this, Bugs Meany!"
cried Sally. "You're so crooked you have
to screw on your socks."

Bugs sniffed. "Kindly tell them, Officer."

Officer Murphy spoke to Encyclopedia.
"Bugs stopped me this morning as I was

driving past the junkyard on my rounds. He said he saw a boy in a red sweater— you—leaning over the oil drum."

"Bugs knows I have only one sweater, this red one," said Encyclopedia. "This is a trick to get even."

"Mr. Dillon, who owns the yard, saw a boy leaning into the barrel at about the same time," said Officer Murphy. "However, he couldn't make out more than the red sweater because of the distance."

"The boy was Bugs in a red sweater pretending to be Encyclopedia," said Sally. "Then Bugs changed to the brown one he has on now before stopping you, Officer."

"This dame is off the wall," said Bugs. "If I changed sweaters, the red one would still be around here. I didn't have time to go home."

"So why are you wearing a girl's brown sweater?" said Sally. "The buttons are on the left side. A boy's sweater has the buttons on the right side."

Bugs looked like a boy who had swallowed a school of goldfish. Finally he stammered, "I—it's my-my girl friend's sweater. I borrowed it this morning."

"What girl friend?" jeered Sally. "On a date, you throw money around like a man in a straitjacket."

Bugs snarled. Sally snarled back. Officer Murphy had to step between them.

Encyclopedia glanced down at his own red sweater. It had stains where he had leaned against the oil drum. The stains on Bug's sweater were different.

Officer Murphy said, "Mr. Dillon didn't see a girl, but Bugs says he saw you, Sally. Bugs claims you two spoke about coming back in an hour to change the hiding place. So I agreed to wait with him and watch."

Bugs clapped his head. "The son of our beloved chief of police is a cheap shoplifter!" he cried. "Oh, the shame of it!"

Sally was shaking with anger. "Encyclopedia, you can't let Bugs get away with this!"

"Don't worry," said Encyclopedia. "He won't."

## WHY NOT?

*(Turn to page 105 for the solution to The Case of the Red Sweater.)*

# The Case of
# the Painting Gerbils

On the day the summer art show opened Mark Reardon trotted into the Brown Detective Agency. He was alone.

Immediately Encyclopedia smelled trouble. Mark seldom went anyplace without Herman and Sherman, his gerbils.

Mark's father ran a training school for pets and always said, "I never met a problem gerbil."

But Encyclopedia guessed that the gerbils had a problem. "Is Herman hurt?" he inquired. "Or Sherman?"

"Just their pride," replied Mark. "They've been insulted. Somebody told on them."

"Told what?" asked Sally.

"That they're gerbils," said Mark.

"Nobody would mistake them for kangaroos," remarked Encyclopedia. "I mean, don't they like being gerbils?"

"Yes, but they want to be artists, too," said Mark. "Read this."

He handed Encyclopedia a newspaper story.

It told about a Texas chimpanzee named Manfred Simpson. Manfred was allowed to throw fruit against a sheet of wood. After a month, the wood was caked with goo. His owner had called the mess "Earth Mother" and had entered it in an art show in Chicago.

"Earth Mother" won first prize. Before the world discovered it was done by an ape, the painting was bought for $15,000 by a museum in New York.

"I get it," said Encyclopedia. "What a chimp can do, two gerbils can do!"

"You better believe it," said Mark. "But somebody told the judges at the art show this morning that Herman Sherman is really two gerbils. The judges wouldn't accept their painting."

"Who told?" asked Sally.

"I'm sure it was either Farnsworth Grant or Jerry Tilson or Scott Wells," said Mark. "They were the only ones besides me and my folks who knew what Herman and Sherman can do."

Mark laid twenty-five cents on the gas can by Encyclopedia.

"I want to hire you to find out which one is the dirty snitch," he said. "All three are my pals—or were. Two days ago they played over at my house. One of them must have stolen a peek at Herman and Sherman's painting."

The detectives went with Mark to his house. Encyclopedia wanted to look at the gerbils' workshop.

Mark led them through the kitchen and into the garage. On the floor was a large piece of plywood covered with many colors. One corner was cut off.

"It's really pretty good for modern art," said Encyclopedia in surprise.

"My dad said most of it is *too* good," replied Mark. "He said that if the judges thought it was beautiful or looked like something, the gerbils wouldn't win a

*On the floor was a large piece of plywood covered with many colors.*

prize. So he sawed off the worst part and entered *that* in the show."

"Your dad knows the secret of modern art," said Encyclopedia.

"I don't understand how the gerbils do it," said Sally.

"You might say they finger-paint it," answered Mark. "I spill cans of different colors on the wood. Then Herman and Sherman slide their paws around. It's their hobby."

"Cleaning them afterward must be hard," said Sally.

"Naw, the paint has a water base," said Mark. "All I do is squirt them with an electric water pick."

"You suspect Farnsworth Grant or Jerry Tilson or Scott Wells of telling on them?" said Encyclopedia. "Why?"

"All three knew Herman and Sherman are artists," said Mark.

He explained that the day before yesterday, the four boys had been together in his sun room.

"Farnsworth and I played Ping-Pong," he said. "Scott watched television. Jerry read. Suddenly Jerry asked what 'misled' meant. We all thought it was the past tense of 'misle.'

"Jerry went into the kitchen and looked up the word in the dictionary that Mom keeps by her cookbooks and shouted back the meaning."

"Jerry could have opened the door to the garage and peeked at the gerbils' painting," said Sally.

"And so could have Scott and Farnsworth," said Mark. "Farnsworth banged his wrist on the edge of the Ping-Pong table. It was just a scratch, but he ran into the kitchen to use the first-aid kit."

"What about Scott?" asked Sally.

"He went last and stayed longest. He wanted a drink of ice water, but he had trouble, he said, getting the ice out of the ice tray."

"So at one time or another, all three boys were alone in the kitchen," mused Sally. "Did they know that the dictionary and the first-aid kit are kept there?"

"Yep, they've used both before," replied Mark.

Sally looked discouraged. "Perhaps the tattletale is someone else completely."

"Uh-uh," said Mark. "Consider this. Each of the three boys had good reason for knocking the gerbils' masterpiece out of the art show. Scott's mother entered a painting, and so did Farnsworth's grandmother and Jerry's sister."

"Being beaten by a pair of gerbils would be hard to take," said Encyclopedia.

Sally sighed. "We don't have one real clue. All three boys had an excuse for going into the kitchen alone."

"But one had a phony excuse," said Encyclopedia.

Sally gasped. "Have you proof?"

"The proof," said Encyclopedia, "is still in the kitchen."

## WHAT WAS THE PROOF?

*(Turn to page 106 for the solution to The Case of the Painting Gerbils.)*

# The Case of
# the Time Capsule

Nothing like the time capsule had ever happened to Idaville.

For months children and grown-ups had thought about what to put into it. They had bought special envelopes and filled them with everything from toys to pictures of Idaville's main streets.

The capsule, loaded with thousands of envelopes, was to be lowered deep into the earth and remain buried for a hundred years.

On the day of the big event, Encyclopedia and Sally hiked to the city golf course.

A large hole had been dug behind the sixth green. The capsule stood beside it, chained to a derrick. More than a hundred persons, including the mayor, were on hand for the ceremony.

"There's been a delay," said Benny Breslin, one of Encyclopedia's closest pals. "The capsule still has room for three hundred more envelopes. You can buy them over at that table for a dollar apiece if you hurry."

It was a bargain. The regular price had been two dollars.

"No, thanks," said Encyclopedia. "I've already filled one with a report of my toughest case. A hundred years from now people will know that even kids fought crime."

"Mine has an essay about pollution," said Sally. "I want my great-grandchildren to know that kids fought for clean air and water."

"Gee, you're neat," exclaimed Benny. "All I put in my envelope was my third-grade report card, the one Dad said should be buried."

Benny walked off to buy another envelope and try again. The detectives strolled toward the time capsule.

"Encyclopedia, there's Abe Smathers. He looks terrible. Do you suppose he's sick?"

Abe was founder and president of the Idaville Riddle Club.

"Abe, are you feeling all right?" asked Sally. "You look awful."

"I always look like this before I faint," said Abe, without raising his head. "What's the best way to get to the hospital?"

"Stand in traffic," answered Encyclopedia.

Abe glanced up. At the sight of the boy detective he made an effort to grin.

"Try this," he said. "What does it mean if you go home and you don't have to do any homework or clean your room?"

"It means you're in the wrong house," said Encyclopedia.

"Drat!" grumbled Abe. He thought hard for a moment. "What is twelve feet tall, has three legs, and—"

"Hold on," said Sally. "If you're well enough to tell riddles, you're well enough to tell us what was wrong with you a minute ago."

*"Abe, are you feeling all right?" asked Sally.*
*"You look awful."*

"My lunch was stolen," said Abe. "I left it under the iron bench over there while I looked at the capsule."

"Maybe you're mistaken, and you left it somewhere else," said Sally.

"No soap," said Abe. "I found my lunch bag in a trash basket. It was empty. I don't mind losing the lunch. It was two bagels with lox. Lox is salty. It makes me thirsty as a horse, and the nearest water fountain is on the fourth green."

Encyclopedia saw the water fountain. It was only about a three-minute walk. "What's the big problem?" he asked.

"I had a time capsule envelope in the bag, too," said Abe.

He explained. Last week he had sent in one envelope with a riddle. But he wasn't happy with it. So he had brought another envelope with a better riddle to the burial ceremony.

"I figured boys and girls of the future would be interested in the riddles of to-day," he said. "My first riddle was, Why is the Statue of Liberty standing in New York Harbor?"

"Because it can't sit down," said Sally.

"Phew! A hundred years from now, that will be four hundred years old."

"It's patriotic, but pretty bad," admitted Abe. "That's why I brought along the second riddle today."

"Get it over with," said Encyclopedia, bracing himself.

"Why is the Statue of Liberty hollow?"

"Why?" said Sally.

"You'd be hollow too if you'd given birth to a nation!" Abe sang. Then he looked grim. "I'd like to catch the little thief!"

"What makes you believe the thief is a kid?" Sally asked.

"No grown-up would steal a lunch bag," said Abe. "Or my riddle."

"You think the thief copied the riddle, bought an envelope, and put it in the time capsule with his name on it?" said Encyclopedia.

"Sure," replied Abe. "I can't use it now. Imagine me, the president of the Idaville Riddle Club, putting in the same riddle as someone else. I'd be ruined!"

"There isn't time, anyway," said Sally.

"See, they've stopped selling envelopes. The ceremony should begin soon."

"I'll hire you to find the thief," said Abe. "I have a clue. My riddle wasn't in any of the trash baskets hereabouts. So the thief must still have it in his pocket—and it has my name on it."

"But, Abe, we can't search every boy and girl here," protested Sally.

"That won't be necessary," said Encyclopedia.

WHAT DID ENCYCLOPEDIA MEAN?

*(Turn to page 107 for the solution to The Case of the Time Capsule.)*

# The Case of
# Freddy the Great

Farnsworth Grant poked his head into the Brown Detective Agency long enough to shout:

"Cuthbert DeVan DeVoe is heading this way, and you should see what he's got!"

"A bad case of fallen arches, I hope," said Sally. Cuthbert DeVan DeVoe was not one of her favorite people.

"Cuthbert means well," said Encyclopedia. "He's just a little stuck up."

"He should be stuck to the ceiling," grumbled Sally. "He thinks he's so much better than anyone else."

The two detectives hastened outside. Cuthbert was walking a gray dog no bigger than a bulldozer. A crowd of children followed at a safe distance.

"That's the biggest, ugliest dog I've ever seen," remarked Encyclopedia.

"That dog would scare an alligator," said Sally. "Do you see his teeth?"

"He must be three parts dragon," answered Encyclopedia.

Cuthbert spotted the detectives and grinned.

"We DeVan DeVoes don't need private detectives to guard our house," he announced. "We have Frederick the Great."

"That's a fancy title for a mutt," said Sally.

"He's named after the famous king of Prussia," said Cuthbert. "His mother was an African wild dog. His father was an Alaskan wolf."

"He looks like he was put together in a junkyard," someone in the crowd called.

Cuthbert stiffened. He glared around. No one moved.

"Frederick the Great is pure killer," warned Cuthbert. "He fears nothing. He can carry an auto tire in his teeth and break wood with his jaws. One word from me, and—"

A cat meowed.

Cuthbert's gaze found Nancy Pringle. She was hugging her cat Juno fearfully.

"Frederick the Great swallows cats whole," said Cuthbert.

Juno and Frederick the Great eyed one another.

The dog bared his teeth. The cat's fur stood on end. Suddenly she hissed, leaped out of Nancy's arms, and landed on Frederick the Great.

The dog yelped in fright and shook her off. He whirled and fled down the block, with Juno hot on his heels.

"You better call him Freddy the Frightened from now on," advised Sally.

Everyone roared with delight except Cuthbert. He had turned red with anger.

"That cat," he cried, "is a gone goose if Frederick the Great gets her in the house. He doesn't eat cats outdoors."

Nancy Pringle let out a wail and ran after the two animals. Cuthbert ran after Nancy.

Half an hour later Nancy came into the Brown Detective Agency. She put a quarter on the gas can beside Encyclopedia.

"I want to hire you," she said. "Cuthbert has Juno and won't give her back!"

She explained. Juno had chased Frederick the Great into Cuthbert's backyard, which was enclosed by a wire fence. Cuthbert had gone into the yard and shut the gate, keeping Nancy out.

"Then Cuthbert opened the back door of the house," said Nancy. "The dog raced inside and Juno followed. Cuthbert went inside, too, and slammed the door. I haven't seen Juno since!"

Sally looked worried. "This could be serious," she said. "Cuthbert is so mad he might hurt Juno."

The detectives and Nancy hurried to Cuthbert's house. He was standing in the backyard as if waiting for them.

"We've come for Juno," said Sally. "We know you have her."

"Your tongue is working overtime," sneered Cuthbert. "I let that stupid cat out the back door to save her life. Frederick

*The dog raced inside and Juno followed. Cuthbert
slammed the door behind them.*

the Great is a terror when he defends his house."

"Applesauce!" said Nancy. "Where is my Juno?"

"She jumped over the fence," said Cuthbert. He pointed to three boxes arranged like stairs by the fence. "See for yourselves."

The detectives and Nancy entered the yard and stepped close to the boxes. Nearby was a large muddy spot. The paw prints of a cat were on each box.

"I can tell if Juno made the prints," said Nancy. "She broke the claw on the fifth toe of her left front paw last week."

"There aren't any claw marks," said Sally.

"That cat was scared and running fast," said Cuthbert. "Maybe cats don't always run with their claws out."

"He may be right," admitted Nancy.

"I still don't think Juno made those prints," said Sally. She stared hard at Cuthbert. "Tell us what you've done with her, or I'll pin your ears back."

"Easy, Sally," cautioned Encyclopedia.

Cuthbert was two years older and a head taller.

"Don't worry," said Cuthbert. "I've boxed a bit. I believe I can deal with her like a gentleman and not do her bodily harm."

Cuthbert, however, didn't fight like a gentleman. In fact, after swinging and missing, he didn't fight at all. Sally knocked him flat with two fast rights to the jaw.

Encyclopedia stepped over Cuthbert and studied the paw prints on the three boxes.

Eleven of the prints showed Juno's five toes clearly. The twelfth print was unclear.

"Cuthbert's pride has taken enough of a beating today," Encyclopedia said to Sally. "When he wakes up, he'll tell us where he's hidden Juno."

## WHAT WAS CUTHBERT'S MISTAKE?

*(Turn to page 108 for the solution to The Case of Freddy the Great.)*

# The Case of
# the Tennis Racket

John Stanley, Idaville's best young tennis player, came into the Brown Detective Agency. He was smiling on one side of his face.

"I've got good news and bad news," he said.

"The good news first," urged Sally.

"I just opened a can of tennis balls. They're number eights."

He explained. A can held three balls. Balls from the same can bore the same number, like two or six or eight, and the manufacturer's name.

"Eight is my lucky number," said John. "I've never lost a match playing with number-eight balls."

"And the bad news?" said Encyclopedia.

"At two o'clock I have to play Ike Quilp in the semifinals of the county-club championships. Ike Quilp is the kid brother of Rowdy Quilp, one of Bugs Meany's Tigers."

John backhanded a quarter onto the table in front of Encyclopedia.

"I want to hire you to keep an eye on things," he said. "It isn't nice to speak bad of anyone, even Tigers, but—"

"Don't apologize," said Sally. "The only way the Tigers can hear anything good about themselves is to talk to each other."

The three children biked off to the country club. John carried two tennis rackets, a towel, and the can of balls in his handlebar basket.

At the club he took out the rackets, the towel, and the balls, but left the empty can behind.

"It's bad luck to take the can along," he said. "Last year, the only match I lost was when I brought a can to the court."

The tournament officials had set up a long table outside the pro shop. Boys and girls were lined up in front of it.

"I have to report in," said John. "See you in a while."

For ten minutes the detectives wandered by themselves, watching the matches already underway. John was entered in the "boys ten-and-under" group.

"There's Fremont Smith with Bugs Meany," said Sally.

Fremont was thirteen and lived on Sally's block. He spied the detectives and walked over to them.

"Are you a tennis fan?" asked Encyclopedia.

"Hardly," replied Fremont. "I can't tell a racket from a rolling pin. But Bugs Meany wants me to join his service club, the Tigers."

"*Service* club?" gasped Sally. "Their only service is repainting the bikes they steal!"

"Bugs said the Tigers do a lot of good deeds," protested Fremont. "Today they're helping out as judges. Bugs suggested that I come here and see for myself."

Before Sally could answer, John came running up.

"Somebody stole my racket and tennis balls!" he cried.

When he caught his breath, he told what had happened.

"Before I got in the line to report to the officials," he said, "I put my towel, tennis balls, and both rackets on a counter in the pro shop. The balls and my lighter-weight racket were gone when I returned for them.

"I don't mind so much losing the balls," he continued. "But the racket is the one I wanted to use today. These courts are hard and fast. With a light racket, I can take a quicker backswing."

"Whoever knew enough to steal your light racket must know a lot about tennis," said Encyclopedia.

"Using my heavy racket on these fast courts means I'll have to change my timing," said John. "Ike Quilp might beat me."

"We've got to find that racket," said Sally. "But where to look for it?"

"Let's start in the pro shop," said Encyclopedia. "All kinds of sporting goods are sold there. The thief wouldn't draw attention to himself by having a racket and balls."

"Ike Quilp has a great net game," said John. "If he beats me, you can blame those Tigers, the no-good thieves!"

"That's not fair," said Fremont. "The Tigers are all straight shooters. Bugs Meany says so."

"Let's find out," said Encyclopedia.

The pro shop was crowded with buyers and lookers. In one corner Encyclopedia saw a steel basket filled with tennis balls. "What's that?" he asked John.

"The tennis teacher uses those balls when he gives lessons," John answered. "He stores them there when it rains or when all the courts are taken for a tournament, like today."

"I think your new tennis balls might be among them," said the boy detective. "Would you look, Fremont? They're brand-new number eights."

"And they have the manufacturer's name, Wilkins, printed above the number," added John.

While Fremont dug into the basket of practice balls, Encyclopedia found the

*Fremont dug into the basket of practice balls.*

missing tennis racket. It was hanging on the wall, hidden behind four rackets that needed new strings.

Suddenly Fremont held up three balls with the word "Wilkins" and the number 8 printed on them. "Here they are!"

"These two might be mine," said John. "But the third ball is too old. Mine were never used."

Fremont looked disappointed. He continued hunting.

"Fremont could be the thief," Sally whispered to Encyclopedia. "Bugs Meany gives every boy who wants to become a Tiger some test of dishonesty."

"You don't sound very certain," said Encyclopedia.

"Maybe John hid the racket and balls himself," said Sally. "Then he'd have an excuse if he lost to Ike Quilp. I just don't know. . . ."

"You will," said Encyclopedia, "if you stop and think."

### WHOM DID ENCYCLOPEDIA SUSPECT?

*(Turn to page 109 for the solution to The Case of the Tennis Racket.)*

# The Case of
# the Fifty Mosquitoes

Sunday afternoon, Encyclopedia and Sally biked to South Park to watch the Odd-Ball Olympics.

Boys and girls from all over Idaville had entered. The games were open to any child under thirteen who could do a crazy stunt.

The detectives reached the park shortly after the judging had begun. They leaned their bikes against a tree and joined the crowd around Rosemary Williams.

Rosemary was blowing "The Missouri Waltz" on her left arm.

"A girl has never won," said Sally. "Maybe Rosemary will."

"No chance," said Pete McGrane, who was standing nearby. Pete was fifteen and an official timekeeper. "Rosemary is nervous. She missed a note on her elbow and two more on her wrist."

The judges agreed with Pete. They gave Rosemary only five points. A perfect score was ten.

"Don't lose hope," Pete said to Sally. "Plenty of other girls are competing."

"Hattie Grossman is our best bet now," said Sally. "Hattie plans to recite 'What Is So Rare As a Day in June' backward."

"Bad news," said Pete. "She tried five minutes ago. Halfway through she got the hiccups. She wiped out."

"Then it's up to Lindylou Duckworth," said Sally stubbornly.

"Maybe," said Pete. "But a lot of boys are good, and don't count out Stinky Redmond."

"Stinky Redmond!" howled Sally. "Ugh!"

Last year Stinky had imitated a blizzard by shaking dandruff out of his hair.

"The stunt didn't make too many parents happy," said Encyclopedia.

"Bugs Meany thought it was great," said Pete. "Bugs says Stinky should start a summer ski camp near his pillow."

"What is Stinky going to do this year?" asked Sally.

"He was *supposed* to take a shower in six seconds," replied Pete.

"Towel and soap included?" gasped Sally.

"Yup," said Pete. "A lot of mothers complained about the stunt last year. They said it was awful. So he promised to do something clean. But he won't."

"Why not?" inquired Sally.

"Because there is no shower in the park," said Pete. "Instead, he's going to swat mosquitoes."

Sally frowned. "There aren't any mosquitoes around."

"That's the hard part of his stunt," said Pete. "First he'll have to coax them here by buzzing like a female laying eggs. Then he'll use a flyswatter—*swissh-splat!* He said he'll down fifty mosquitoes in one hour."

"Yuk!" exclaimed Sally. "Dandruff was cleaner."

"You're wrong," said Pete. "Mosquitoes spread some of the worst diseases, like yellow fever. Killing a mosquito is in the public interest."

"I don't see Stinky anywhere," remarked Encyclopedia.

"He's over there." Pete pointed to a circle of bushes at the edge of the park. "Stinky said he has to be alone to buzz in mosquitoes. At three o'clock he'll be judged."

For the next forty minutes the two detectives and Pete moved with the judges from stunt to stunt.

Lindylou Duckworth surprised everyone except Sally. Lindylou wrist-wrestled all comers while balancing on a banana peel. She won every time.

The judges gave her nine points.

"She lost a point because she's bigger than the boys she beat," explained Pete. "Still, she's in first place."

"She hasn't won yet," said Encyclopedia. "It's three o'clock and time for Stinky Redmond."

As they walked toward the bushes, Sally said, "Stinky is completely hidden. Who knows what he's been up to!"

*Around and under the picnic table and benches was nothing but dirt and dead mosquitoes.*

"The Odd-Ball Olympics are run on the honor code," Encyclopedia reminded her. "No cheating."

"Who told Stinky?" said Sally. "Even if he were voted Boy of the Hour, I'd watch him every minute."

The judges and onlookers entered the ring of bushes through an opening on the far side. Stinky was lying on a picnic table chewing gum.

"Boy, did I buzz 'em here," he cried. "I whomped so many in the first twenty minutes that I lay down and took a nap. See for yourselves."

Everyone looked. Around and under the picnic table and benches was nothing but dirt and dead mosquitoes.

"Count 'em," said Stinky.

A slight breeze stirred the mosquitoes and chased a bubblegum wrapper toward Encyclopedia. It came to rest six feet from the table, beside an ant hill.

Encyclopedia preferred to watch the ants rather than count mosquitoes. A few of the ants were crawling out of the hole in the center of the hill.

"I've been thinking of selling my services to the Department of Health in Washington," said Stinky. "I just might be the greatest gift to mankind since floating soap."

"The big liar!" whispered Sally. "Lindy-lou Duckworth deserves to win."

"I think so, too," said Encyclopedia.

"Then tell the judges that Stinky cheated," urged Sally. "You can prove he did, can't you?"

"Of course," said Encyclopedia.

## WHAT WAS THE PROOF?

*(Turn to page 110 for the solution to The Case of the Fifty Mosquitoes.)*

# The Case of
# Blue-Point Blackie

Caswell Philpott laid a towel on the floor of the Brown Detective Agency and sat down on it.

"The Lotus Position," he announced proudly, crossing his legs so that the soles of his feet touched his thighs. "In yoga, that's what sitting like this is called.'

"How cute," said Sally.

"Yoga is the science of relaxing the body and clearing the mind," said Caswell. "Every position has a name except the headstand. The headstand is the headstand. I'm still learning it, but it's my favorite position."

85

He got up and folded the towel across his arm.

"Something usually happens when I try a headstand," he said. "Yesterday I spotted a dime under my head. Today I overheard two men talking about robbing somebody."

He explained. While fishing in Mill Pond, he had got the urge to practice a headstand. As he was balancing himself, two men passed on the footpath. They were talking.

"One man said that they'd have to steal Blue-Point Blackie's overnight bag when he arrived by bus this afternoon," said Caswell.

"Who is Blue-Point Blackie, and when is his bus due in?" asked Encyclopedia.

Caswell shrugged. "I didn't hear."

"Well, what did the two men look like?" said Sally.

"They looked upside down," said Caswell. "I was standing on my head."

"Do you think we should telephone your father?" Sally said to Encyclopedia.

The detectives decided against calling

in the police. They hadn't enough facts. Blue-Point Blackie might not be coming to Idaville.

"If you don't call the police, you should do something yourselves," said Caswell. "Blue-Point Blackie sounds like a gangster's name. I'll bet he has stolen money packed in his overnight bag . . . and a gun!"

Encyclopedia wished there were a yoga exercise Caswell could do with his mouth—such as shut it.

"It's only ten minutes to noon," said Sally. "We can hang around the bus station this afternoon and keep our eyes open."

Caswell insisted on coming along. Encyclopedia was soon sorry that he let him. Everyone in the bus-station waiting room looked like a gangster to Caswell.

First it was a man in a tan hat who stood by the magazine rack thumbing through a movie magazine. The man finally bought a newspaper and sat down on a bench.

"See, he's not reading," said Caswell. "He's really watching for Blue-Point Blackie!"

"You overheard *two* men," Sally pointed out.

"What about those two by the soda machine?" said Caswell.

The two men were drinking from paper cups by the soda machine. The taller man glanced at his wristwatch.

"Maybe they're just thirsty," said Encyclopedia.

"Look over by the ticket window," said Caswell. "Those two men in dark suits aren't buying tickets. They're probably asking if Blue-Point Blackie's bus is on time."

"Caswell, is there anyone you don't suspect?" demanded Sally.

"Those two must be big-shot crooks from out of town," said Caswell. "Nobody in Idaville wears dark clothes in summer. You'd better follow them. I'll watch things here."

Encyclopedia and Sally followed the men in the dark suits out to where the buses arrived and departed. Encyclopedia was glad to get away from Caswell.

During the next twenty minutes, buses came and went. Yet the two men in the dark suits remained waiting by the railing.

Encyclopedia lost sight of them when passengers, streaming from the two o'clock bus from Glenn City, blocked his view. Suddenly a woman screamed.

The detectives rushed over. A black-haired man lay on the floor, unconscious. No one seemed to know what had happened to him.

Officer Carlson came hurrying up. "It's Blue-Point Blackie," he said in surprise. "What is a Chicago crook doing in Idaville?"

"If he ever had an overnight bag with him, it's gone now," whispered Sally.

The detectives found Caswell. He could tell them nothing.

"I got bored," he admitted. "So I practiced my headstand."

"You did *what?*" gasped Sally.

"The man in the tan hat folded his newspaper in half and was reading the bottom half," said Caswell. "So the headlines were on my side. I tried reading them while standing on my head. They were upside down, and it took a long time—"

*A black-haired man lay on the floor, unconscious.*

"Never mind the headlines!" cried Sally. "Did you see anyone running away with an overnight bag?"

"Everyone was running after some woman screamed," said Caswell. "That's when the man in the tan hat left the bench. I was just combing my hair when you came back."

"I ought to comb it with a blowtorch," said Sally furiously.

"I think the headlines began, 'Earth-quake Hits . . .'" said Caswell.

"You missed everything trying to read a headline," shrieked Sally. "Blue-Point Blackie was slugged, and we don't have a clue!"

"Oh, yes, we do," corrected Encyclopedia.

### WHAT WAS THE CLUE?

*(Turn to page 111 for the solution to The Case of Blue-Point Blackie.)*

# The Case of
# the Hit-Run Car

Encyclopedia and Sally were walking on a quiet street in downtown Idaville when they heard a screech of tires.

Around a corner roared a blue car. Inside were two men. They looked scared.

The car raced down the block and turned onto Ninth Street.

"They're in a mighty big hurry," said Encyclopedia.

"The driver should be arrested before he kills someone," said Sally angrily.

It had been a peaceful afternoon until then. The detectives had just visited Benny Breslin at Mercy Hospital. Benny's tonsils had been removed.

Suddenly they heard a woman shouting. They ran to Jefferson Place, the street from which the blue car had come.

A woman was standing near the sidewalk. She was shouting at the top of her lungs. "Call an ambulance! Call the police!"

A man lay by a parked car. He was holding his back. His face was twisted with pain.

As if in answer to a prayer, an ambulance sped up. Its lights were blinking and its siren screamed.

The woman stepped into the middle of the street and threw up her arms.

"Stop!" she shouted. "Stop!"

Parked cars narrowed the one-way street, and the ambulance driver could not steer around the woman. He slammed on his brakes.

"Lady, get out of the way!" he pleaded. "We're on a call!"

"Take this man to the hospital," she insisted. "He's been hit by a car!"

The driver tried to argue. He had no time to stop. "A man on Bradley Square has suffered a heart attack," he said.

*The woman stepped into the middle of the street
and threw up her arms. "Stop!" she shouted.*

The woman held her ground in the middle of the street. "What's the matter with you? This man's hurt!"

The injured man protested. "Let them answer their call," he said. "Mercy Hospital is only two blocks away. I can make it."

"Don't you try!" scolded the woman. "Crazy drivers! Crazy ambulances!"

By now a large crowd of men and women had gathered to watch. They seemed to side with the excited woman.

"Okay, okay, lady, you win," the ambulance driver said, shaking his head. "This could cost me my job, but I guess there is room."

He nodded to his partner and both men got out of the ambulance, their white uniforms bright spots of comfort. They opened the back doors and reached for a wheeled stretcher.

"Heck, I don't need that," said the injured man.

"Yes, you do," said the woman. "The blue car knocked you six feet. I saw it. Oh, I wish I'd got the license number!"

So did Encyclopedia. He had glimpsed only the last part—008.

The two men in white were carrying the stretcher when more sirens sounded. Four police cars halted behind the ambulance.

Chief Brown leaned out of the first car. "Move that ambulance to one side," he commanded.

As the ambulance was being moved, Chief Brown spied Encyclopedia. "What are you doing here, Leroy?" he called.

"We were visiting Benny Breslin at Mercy Hospital," replied Encyclopedia. "This man was struck down by a speeding car."

"Did you see it happen?"

"No," said Encyclopedia. "But I'm pretty certain I saw the car that hit him."

"Are you chasing it?" asked Sally.

"Chasing robbers," said Chief Brown. "The First City Bank was held up ten minutes ago. The bank teller who phoned the station was still so scared she didn't know how many robbers there were. She remembered only that they wore masks and long black capes."

The ambulance had pulled into an open parking space. Chief Brown sent the other police cars on to the bank.

"The hit-run car might be the getaway car," he said. "The bank is only six blocks from here. The robbers would come this way to dodge heavy traffic. What did the car look like?"

"It was a blue four-door Chevrolet, with two men in it," said Encyclopedia. "The last three numbers of the license plate are oh-oh-eight."

"That will help," said Chief Brown. "Who saw the accident?"

"I guess that woman—and the man on the stretcher."

Chief Brown spoke with the woman and the man. He returned to the police car and used the two-way radio.

Meanwhile, the men in white were lifting the injured man into the ambulance. They had strapped him down and were gently rolling him in feet first. Encyclopedia could see the top of his head clearly. It was bald, with cuts that were bleeding slightly.

Encyclopedia thought about the man's head. He thought about the blue car and the men in white. He thought about the woman who had stopped the ambulance.

Chief Brown had finished talking on the radio.

"You're our best witness," he said to Encyclopedia. "Neither the injured man nor the woman even recalls how many doors the blue car had. I'm afraid the robbers will take a lot of time to catch."

"No, Dad," said Encyclopedia. "You can make an arrest right now."

WHAT DID ENCYCLOPEDIA MEAN?

*(Turn to page 112 for the solution to The Case of the Hit-Run Car.)*

## Solution to *The Case of the Midnight Visitor*

Mr. Butler didn't dare write down the name of the kidnapper. The kidnapper might have seen it. So he wrote the number 7891011.

If that had been the *entire* clue, however, he would have written it on the pad by the telephone and not on the calendar.

Encyclopedia saw that the number stood for the 7th, 8th, 9th, 10th, and 11th months of the year—July, August, September, October, November. Taking the first letter of each month, he discovered that Mr. Butler had written JASON.

That night Chief Brown questioned Arthur Jason, who secretly (and unjustly) blamed Mr. Butler for his business troubles. Jason broke down and led the police to the garage where Mr. Butler was being held.

### Solution to *The Case of the Hidden Penny*

Bugs had seen Encyclopedia and Elmo enter the restaurant before they had seen him. He guessed why they had come.

So he hid the penny in his hot dog. To cover it, he had quickly heaped sauerkraut on top and *then* smeared on mustard. That was his mistake!

No hot-dog lover smears mustard on *top* of sauerkraut. The mustard goes on *first* and the sauerkraut afterward.

Bugs had expected Encyclopedia to search him and then leave. But Encyclopedia didn't.

So rather than have to swallow the last part of the hotdog—the part with the penny—Bugs gave the coin back to Elmo.

## Solution to *The Case of the Red Sweater*

Bugs wasn't wearing a girl's sweater, as Sally thought.

Encyclopedia realized that Bugs was wearing his sweater inside out!

One side was red. The other side was brown. The sweater could be worn either side out.

Bugs wore it red side out when he leaned over the oil drum to make Mr. Dillon believe he was Encyclopedia.

The oil stains looked "different," however, when it was worn with the brown side out. And the buttons were then on the left side, like a girl's.

Bugs's father paid for the things Bugs and his Tigers had stolen in order to frame the two detectives.

**Solution to *The Case of the Painting Gerbils***

The dictionary was the proof.

"Misled" is not the past tense of "misle." There is no such word as "misle" in the dictionary.

Yet Jerry called back the meaning to the boys. So he knew what the word meant before he walked into the kitchen.

"Misled" is the past tense of "mislead," which means "to lead in the wrong direction."

Jerry was the snitch. He went into the kitchen so that he could open the door to the garage and see what Herman and Sherman's painting looked like.

Thus he was able to tell the judges which painting was done by the gerbils.

"Lox is salty. It makes you thirsty as a horse," said Abe.

So Encyclopedia kept an eye on the water fountain on the fourth green. One boy made three trips to drink.

On his fourth trip, the detectives and Abe stopped him. He was a blue-eyed fourth grader named Rockwell Harrison III.

Rockwell admitted eating the lox and bagels and taking the riddle. "So what?" he sneered.

What, indeed? The detectives left Rockwell to Abe and walked away.

Abe caught up with them later. He blew on his fist.

"What has two blue eyes and one of them is black?" he asked.

## Solution to *The Case of Freddy the Great*

Cuthbert had tried to make it look as if Juno had escaped from his backyard by climbing the boxes and jumping over the fence.

He had picked up Juno by the hind legs. Then he had dipped her front paws in the muddy spot.

Next, he had lowered her on the boxes so as to leave the right amount of paw prints. All the prints had five toes.

But cats have five toes on their front paws only. Their back paws have four.

Cuthbert didn't know that. But Encyclopedia did!

Trapped by his own mistake, Cuthbert returned Juno unharmed.

## Solution to *The Case of the Tennis Racket*

The guilty boy was Fremont, who pretended to know nothing about tennis. Thus, no one would suspect him of knowing which tennis racket to steal.

He deliberately picked out the wrong ball, an old Wilkins number 8, along with two new ones, from the steel basket.

That was his mistake!

If he really knew nothing about tennis, he could not have known how many balls—three—came in a can. Furthermore, no one told him how many balls were stolen.

Fremont confessed. The theft had been a test to prove himself fit to be a Tiger. He flunked it, and John beat Ike Quilp.

### Solution to *The Case of the Fifty Mosquitoes*

Stinky boasted that he had needed only the first twenty minutes of the hour given to him to buzz in and kill the mosquitoes.

However, had the mosquitoes really been on the ground for forty minutes, the ants would have found them. Instead, the ants were just coming out of their hole six feet from the table!

When Encyclopedia pointed this out, Stinky admitted he had brought dead mosquitoes with him to the bushes. He had scattered them when he saw the judges approaching.

Stinky was given a score of 0, and Lindylou Duckworth was declared the winner of the Odd-Ball Olympics.

## Solution to *The Case of Blue-Point Blackie*

The man in the tan hat was only making believe he was reading his newspaper.

When a newspaper is read with the top half folded over, the headlines appear upside down.

To Caswell, who was standing on his head, the headline should have been right side up. Instead, they were upside down!

Hence, Encyclopedia realized the man was a lookout.

Encyclopedia remembered the movie magazine which the man had handled. The police lifted fingerprints from it.

Blue-Point Blackie had been carrying stolen diamonds in his overnight bag. Members of a rival gang jumped him.

With the help of the fingerprints, the gang was rounded up within two weeks.

## Solution to *The Case of the Hit-Run Car*

The robbers had worn hospital uniforms beneath their black capes and used a stolen ambulance as the getaway car.

They had planned everything—except the mischance of passing an accident.

They could not run over the shouting woman or ignore her pleas without drawing attention to themselves.

Still, they might have got away, but for Encyclopedia. He realized they weren't really ambulance men. They loaded the injured man into the ambulance feet first.

All life-support equipment is stored behind the front seat of an ambulance. So patients are always loaded *head first!*

P.S. Aided by the license plate numbers which Encyclopedia had seen, the police caught the hit-run driver as well.

## ABOUT THE AUTHOR

Since the publication of the first *Encyclopedia Brown* book in 1963, DONALD J. SOBOL has written roughly one book a year. In 1967, at a Children's Book Fair, he explained, "I began writing children's mysteries because the mystery element was really very small in the so-called mysteries that were written for children and I felt that this was a shame." In 1976, the *Encyclopedia Brown* series was the recipient of a special 1976 Edgar Allan Poe Award, presented by the Mystery Writers of America in recognition of these books as the first mysteries that millions of children read. In addition to the *Encyclopedia Brown* series, Mr. Sobol has authored over twenty books for young readers. A native of New York, he now lives in Florida with his wife and children. He has been a free-lance writer for eighteen years.

# Bantam Skylark Paperbacks
## *The Kid-Pleasers*

Especially designed for easy reading with large type, wide margins and captivating illustrations, Skylarks are "kid-pleasing" paperbacks featuring the authors, subjects and characters children love.

| | | |
|---|---|---|
| 15097 | CHARLIE AND THE CHOCOLATE FACTORY Roald Dahl | $2.75 |
| 15097 | CHARLIE AND THE GREAT GLASS ELEVATOR Roald Dahl | $1.95 |
| 15113 | JAMES AND THE GIANT PEACH Roald Dahl | $2.50 |
| 15100 | ENCYCLOPEDIA BROWN BOY DETECTIVE Donald Sobol | $1.50 |
| 15026 | ENCYCLOPEDIA BROWN CASE OF THE SECRET PITCH Donald Sobol | $1.25 |
| 15060 | ABEL'S ISLAND William Steig | $1.95 |
| 15106 | BIG RED Jim Kjelgaard | $2.25 |
| 15067 | DRAGON, DRAGON AND OTHER TALES John Gardner | $1.75 |
| 15089 | A DREAM FOR ADDIE Gail Rock | $1.95 |
| 15050 | EMILY UPHAM'S REVENGE     Avi | $1.50 |
| 15008 | IRISH RED: SON OF BIG RED Jim Kjelgaard | $1.95 |
| 15086 | JACOB TWO-TWO MEETS THE HOODED FANG Mordecai Richler | $1.95 |
| 15050 | THE EYES OF THE AMARYLLIS Natalie Babbitt | $1.75 |
| 15065 | TUCK EVERLASTING Natalie Babbitt | $1.95 |

Buy them at your local bookstore or use this handy coupon for ordering:

---

**Bantam Books, Inc., Dept. EB, 414 East Golf Road, Des Plaines, Ill. 60016**

Please send me the books I have checked above. I am enclosing $_____ (please add $1.25 to cover postage and handling). Send check or money order—no cash or C.O.D.'s please.

Mr/Mrs/Miss _____

Address _____

City _____ State/Zip _____

SK–3/81

Please allow four to six weeks for delivery. This offer expires 9/81

---

# MS READ-a-thon-
## a simple way
## to start youngsters reading.

Boys and girls between 6 and 14 can join the MS READ-a-thon and help find a cure for Multiple Sclerosis by reading books. And they get two rewards—the enjoyment of reading, and the great feeling that comes from helping others.

Parents and educators: For complete information call your local MS chapter, or call toll-free (800) 243-6000. Or mail the coupon below.

# Kids can help, too!